For my mother,
whose hand guided my first encounter
with the caiman and with life.

—M. E. M.

To Uncle Melo,
who told us this story when we were children.
I didn't believe him. No one did.

—R. P.

BY MARÍA EUGENIA MANRIQUE ◗ ILLUSTRATED BY RAMÓN PARÍS

Translated by AMY BRILL

the Caiman

amazon crossing kids

This story happened many years ago in San Fernando de Apure, a tiny city on the bank of a wide river that was home to many alligators. Their skins were highly prized by hunters, who sometimes left young, orphaned alligators behind.

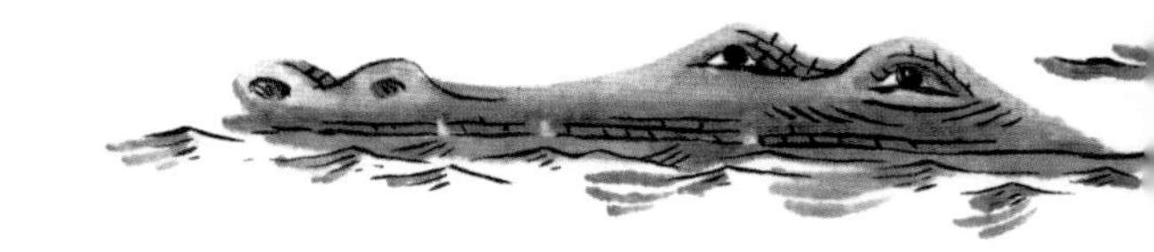

One day, during a game of hide-and-seek, a little girl named Julia found one of these baby alligators—a river caiman—wandering around the riverbank. The discovery caused a commotion, and the children passed the tiny reptile around.

But when it was time to go home, none of them was brave enough to take the baby along. Julia was about to put it back in the river when Faoro, the town jeweler and watchmaker who lived on 24th of July Street, approached. Faoro picked up the baby alligator, which was no bigger than the palm of his hand, stroked her gently, and, without another thought, slid her into the front pocket of his shirt.

"Don't worry," he told the children. "I'm going to bring her home and take care of her. You can come and play with her whenever you like."

When he got home, Faoro peeked inside his pocket. The creature slept peacefully, curled up like a clock spring. Because her skin was very dark, Faoro decided to name her Night.

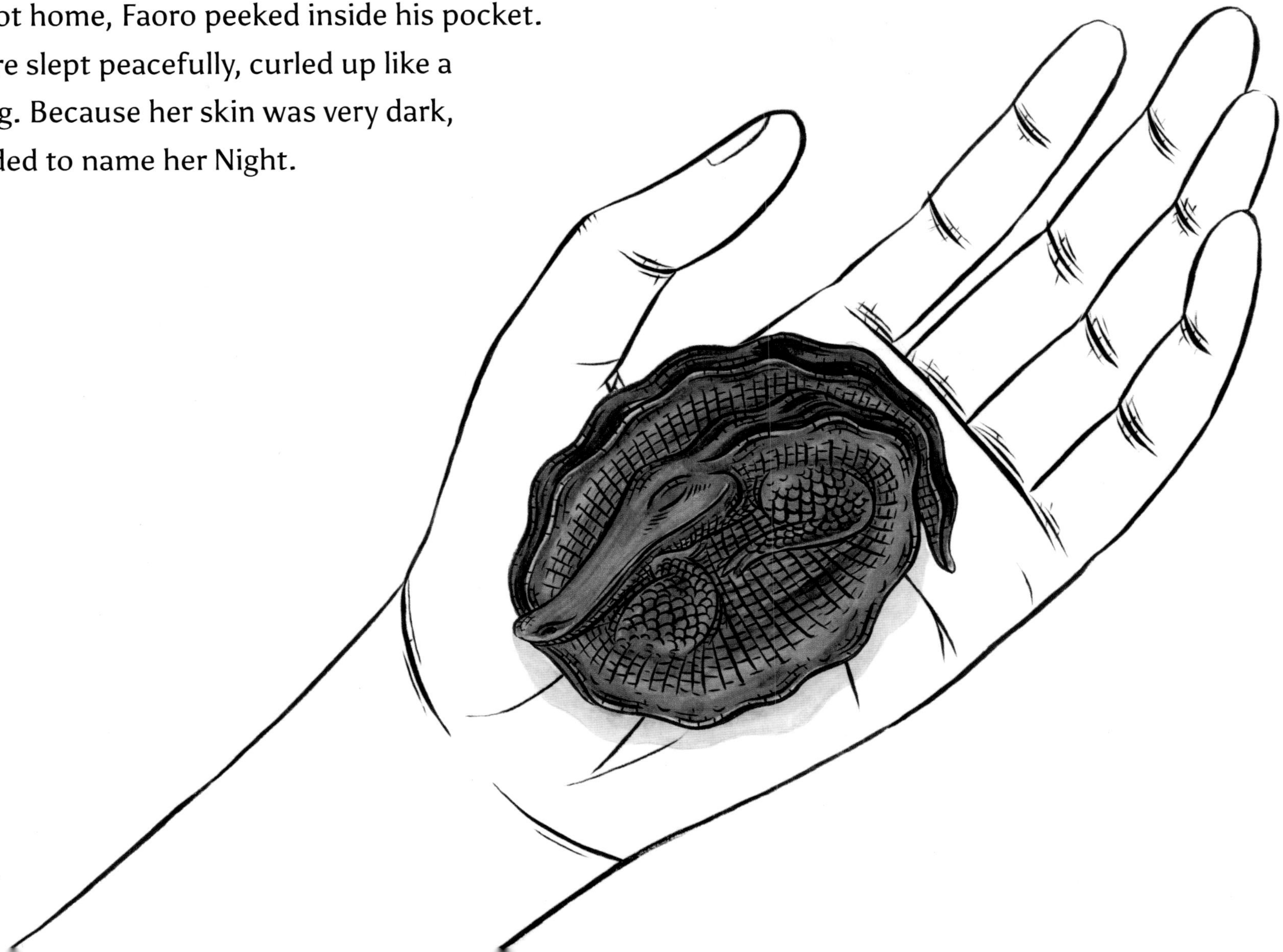

Faoro took Night to his workshop with him each day.

News of the young clockmaker who had adopted a baby alligator traveled quickly, and visitors began arriving at the workshop from all the nearby villages and towns. They brought cracked clocks, broken necklaces, bracelets for engraving, and rings for resizing. They stood in line in the street and waited their turn to see and touch the little alligator.

JOYERIA

So Night got used to people, especially Faoro. She followed him everywhere. Each morning, Night climbed into Faoro's bed to wake him up by resting her head on his lap.

Faoro said good morning with a gentle pat on the caiman's head.

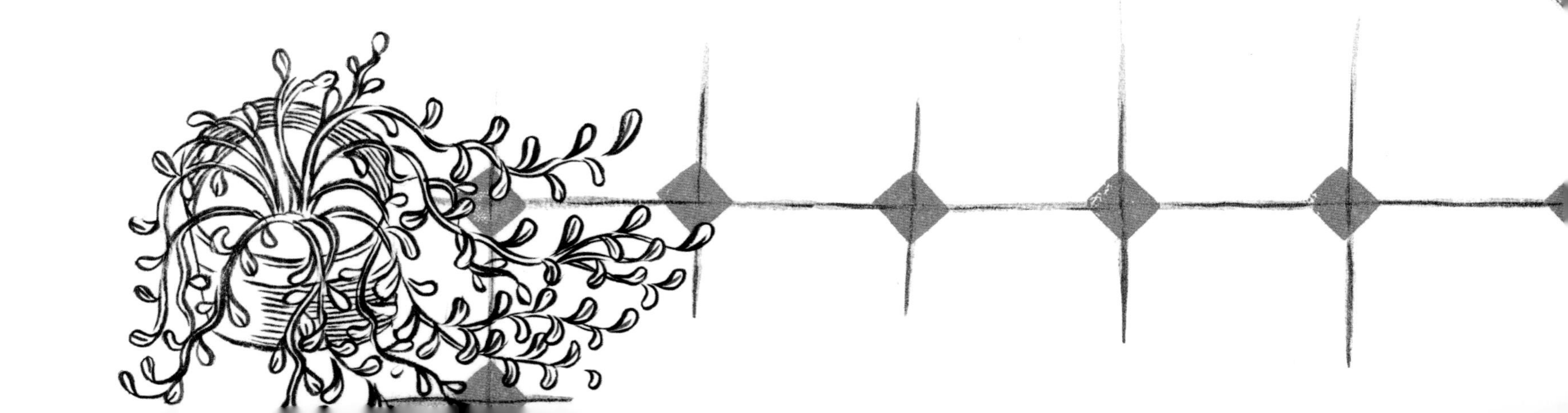

River caimans need freshwater to live, so Faoro built a pond with a slope in the backyard for Night to come and go as she pleased.

The caiman liked her pond. She laid hundreds of tiny eggs in the water, and played with the neighborhood children, who visited often.

Time passed.

The alligator was more than six feet long when Faoro told her he was in love with his neighbor, Angela, whom he had met at the town fair. He wanted to marry her, but had to be sure that Angela and Night would get along.

At their first meeting, Night wrapped herself around Faoro's legs and stared at Angela. Angela was terrified. But Faoro took her hands between his own, and together they stroked the alligator's head.

Night closed her eyes as if she were smiling.

They set a date for the wedding.

Faoro made the wedding rings and a small surprise for Night: gold settings for her fangs. The alligator showed them off to the delight of all the guests.

From the moment Angela arrived, life was joyful. Angela sang and laughed. She served delicious cakes and cookies and fresh juice to all the children who came to play with the alligator.

Years passed. Night grew until she was ten feet long.
Ten feet of a quiet and happy life.

One hot summer afternoon, Faoro got sick. Angela stopped singing. The house was full of sadness. Night would not leave Faoro's side.

When it was time to say goodbye, the alligator laid her head on Faoro's lap.

His touch was reassuring. "Night, I have to go, but don't be afraid," he whispered. "Everything will be all right. Be a friend to Angela. She loves you and will always take care of you."

A great desolation settled upon the house. Even the parrots and parakeets fell quiet. The caiman slowly crossed the silent backyard. She went into a small storage room full of old things. And there she stayed, not leaving, not eating.

In her grief, Angela worried about Night but could not find a way to make her come out or eat anything.

Days, then weeks, went by.

One morning, Angela was sorting papers and found a card Faoro had written many years earlier. It said:

> *Dear Angela,*
> *Your beautiful voice fills my heart with joy.*
> *Whenever you sing, I feel you close.*

Thinking of him, Angela began to sing.

Night's head appeared. Step by step, she emerged and stood in the backyard, listening, her great jaws open, gathering light and warmth from the sun.

From that day on, the children returned to play with the caiman.

And Angela never stopped singing.

María Eugenia Manrique is one of the girls portrayed in this story. She rode the caiman when she visited her family in San Fernando de Apure. She was born in Caracas, Venezuela, and currently lives in Barcelona, Spain. She studied fine art in Mexico City, specializing in xylography and engraving; Eastern painting at Nankín University, China; and sumi-e and calligraphy at the Nihon Shuji Kyoiku Zaidan Foundation in Japan. Her work has been exhibited in museums and galleries in Venezuela, Spain, Mexico, Colombia, the United States, Puerto Rico, China, Italy, Argentina, and Japan. In 2014 she won the Grand Prize in Eastern Painting at the International Chinese Painting and Calligraphy Exposition at the Anshan Museum in China. She has published four books on Eastern painting. *The Caiman* is her first children's book.

Ramón París was born in Caracas, Venezuela, and as a child lived in Barinas, a plains state like Apure, where he also heard the story of the caiman. He currently lives in Barcelona, Spain. His first book for children, *Un abuelo, sí*, was followed by *Un perro en casa, Estaba la rana*, and most recently *Duermevela*, which was selected for the Bologna Book Fair Illustrator's exhibition. His books have been recognized with honors including Los Mejores del Banco del Libro award; the IBBY Honour List; Fundación Cuatrogatos; and White Ravens, and have been translated into Chinese, Portuguese, French, Catalan, Korean, German, and now English. He works to create a unique atmosphere for every story he illustrates, because each one speaks to him in a different voice.

PHOTO © EDGAR MORENO

José Faoro was born in Italy and moved to San Fernando de Apure, Venezuela, when he was fifteen years old. He opened a jewelry store on the 24th of July Street that made him famous. In addition to repairing jewelry and clocks, he prepared natural medicines, including a special concoction to help cattle gain weight.

They say his house was filled with animals: a crane that flew in and out every day and even let Faoro comb his feathers, porcupines that went for walks with him, a rescued jaguar, and a wild cat.

Faoro found the caiman when she was only three days old and called her Negro, which means *black* in Spanish. He loved her like a spoiled child. While he worked, the caiman rested at his feet and only slept in his room, even after he married his beloved neighbor, Angela. Black ate about 6.5 pounds (3 kg) of meat, or fish from the sea—never the river—every day, using the gold fangs Faoro had made for her. In 1972 Faoro died of a heart attack. They say that when the urn was placed in the living room for the service, Black jumped onto it and no one could remove her. They say she spent four months without eating, but went on to live for another twenty years. She died in 1992 of a heart attack, just like her beloved Faoro.

Previously published as *La caimana* by Ediciones Ekaré in Venezuela in 2019. Translated from Spanish by Amy Brill. First published in English by Amazon Crossing Kids in collaboration with Amazon Crossing in 2021.

Published by Amazon Crossing Kids, New York, in collaboration with Amazon Crossing

www.apub.com

ISBN-13: 9781542031585 (hardcover)
ISBN-10: 1542031583 (hardcover)

The illustrations were rendered using Copic markers, Chinese ink-brush, and digital media.

Book design adapted by Abby Dening

Printed in China
First Edition

10 9 8 7 6 5 4 3 2 1